TOM PERCIVAL

Little Legends

THE GENIE'S CURSE

...m Percival grew up in a remote and ...autiful part of south Shropshire. It was ... remote that he lived in a small caravan ...ithout mains electricity or any sensible ...rm of heating. He thinks he's probably ...ne of the few people in his peer group to ...ave learned to read by gas lamp.

Having established a career as a ...icture-book author and illustrator, Little ...egends is Tom's first chapter-book series ...or young readers. The idea for Little Legends was developed by Tom with Made in Me, a digital studio exploring new ways for technology and storytelling to inspir...

MACM...

This book is dedicated to
Joshua and Zachary for saying,
'Whaʌaat?!'

First published 2016 by Macmillan Children's Books
an imprint of Pan Macmillan
20 New Wharf Road, London N1 9RR
Associated companies throughout the world
www.panmacmillan.com

ISBN 978-1-4472-9213-5

3 5 7 9 8 6 4 2

A CIP catalogue record for this book is available from the British Library.

Printed and bound by CPI Group (UK) Ltd, Croydon CR0 4YY

Contents

1

Fairy Dreamboat

Ella sat under the Story Tree and gazed up at the gold and silver branches. Each one contained a record of every story that had *ever* been told near it. To 'read' one, all you had to do was touch a branch or a leaf and the story would spring to life in your head. Somewhere up there was the tale of how she and Cole, her Fairy Godbrother, had been rescued from

an *awfully* wicked witch by Red, Jack, Anansi and Rapunzel.

Ella smiled as she looked at her new friends and picked up a sock with a hole in it that needed darning – so many chores, so little time!

'Hey, Ella,' said Rapunzel. 'Can I have my foot back, please?'

'Oh! Sorry!' replied Ella, dropping Rapunzel's foot. 'Was I doing it again?'

Everybody nodded. Ella had a habit of fixing *anything* that looked broken, ripped, dirty or torn – even if it didn't need it. Like the time that she'd sewn up all the holes in Anansi's favourite jumper – including the neck and both arms.

'It isn't Ella's fault!' protested Cole.

'The wicked witch cast a spell on Ella that makes her want to fix everything – but I can't reverse it, the magic is too strong.'

'Isn't there anyone –'

'– else who could help?' asked Hansel and Gretel, who often finished each other's sentences, meals and crossword puzzles.

'**Whaaaat?**' squawked Jack's magical talking hen, Betsy.

'I don't think the magic set I was given for my birthday would do the trick,' replied Jack. 'You *can* use it to make it look like your finger's been chopped off though!'

'Cool!' said Anansi.

'**Whaaaat?**' screeched Betsy again.

Although she *was* a talking hen, the only word that Betsy could actually say was 'what', but somehow Jack always seemed to understand her.

'Good idea!' said Jack. He turned to Anansi. 'What about your Uncle Rufaro? He understands magic, doesn't he?'

'Yeah, but he's not here at the moment,' said Anansi. 'He's still trying to break the curse on . . . you know . . .' Anansi shrugged, trying not to look too upset that most of his family had been cursed to look like trolls. 'He should be back by tomorrow night though,' he added.

WHAAAT!!!

'That reminds me!' said Jack. 'Have you seen the posters that Mayor Fitch has been putting up? Telling everyone to report any troll sightings? Well, the troll on the poster looks *exactly* like Rufaro.'

'You mean *those* posters?' said Anansi, pointing to the noticeboard which was plastered with them. 'They're *everywhere*! I was standing still earlier and nearly had one pinned to my back!'

'**Whaaat!**' interrupted Betsy.

'Well, yes, Mayor Fitch *does* seem a *bit* mean . . .' replied Jack. 'But he *is* the mayor of Tale Town, so we shouldn't be *too* rude!'

'I think we're getting off-topic here,' interrupted Rapunzel. 'Right now we need to work out what to do about *Ella*.' Everyone watched Ella trying to sweep the dust off a small pile of dirt.

'What about one of the other fairies, Cole?' asked Red. 'Like your Fairy Grandmother, or Fairy Half-Cousin? Do you think any of them could help?'

'They're all off at some big Fairy Folk meeting,' said Cole. 'But there *is* my Fairy Big Brother, Zak . . . He's pretty much amazing at, well . . .

everything – but he likes *everyone* to know it too.'

'Can you, like, summon him or something?' asked Rapunzel.

'I guess,' muttered Cole. 'But don't blame *me* if he just goes on and on about how great he is.' He clicked his fingers and a cup with a string poking out of the back appeared in mid-air next to him. He leaned forward and spoke into it.

'Zak? Hello? Yeah, hi, it's me Cole . . .' He paused and listened to the muffled sound which came out of the cup.

'Yes, *of course* your little brother!' Cole rolled his eyes. 'How many other Coles do you know?' He paused again and listened to the cup.

'Look, can you just *please* come over? I've got a bit of a—'

There was a bright blue flash and suddenly another fairy was standing next to Cole. They looked very similar, with the same bright blue glow, except *this* boy was older and taller. His hair flopped down over his eyes and his collar was turned up.

'Hey,' said Zak casually, brushing his hair away from his face. 'So, you kids need a hand or something?'

'It's Ella,' replied Cole, nodding at his friend as she tried to sew a petal back on to a daisy. 'She's under a spell that makes her want to fix everything. Do you think you can lift it?'

Zak narrowed his eyes

thoughtfully and stared off into the distance.

Rapunzel, Gretel and Ella all sighed. Cole rolled his eyes.

'I *can* help,' Zak said eventually, sweeping back his messy fringe.

'Really?' cooed Rapunzel.

'You're *so* clever!' breathed Gretel.

'Can I touch your hair?' added Ella, and then blushed.

Zak smiled to himself. 'In fact, I'll

go one better . . . How about I make it so that all magic just bounces off Ella? That way *no* spells or curses will have *any* effect on her at all!'

'Could you *really* do that?' asked Rapunzel.

'Wow!' exclaimed Gretel.

'That would be *AMAZING*!' added Ella.

'No worries,' said Zak, then bent down close to Cole. 'It's pretty simple though,' he whispered, in the kind of whisper that's loud enough for everyone to hear. 'I'd have thought even *you* could do it . . .'

Blue sparks fizzed out of Cole's hair. 'Just get on with it,' he muttered.

Zak stood up and smiled as a bright

blue ring of light appeared around Ella. She looked down in surprise as the light whirled around her, sparkling and shimmering before it shrank down into a blue glass necklace that tied itself around her neck.

'Done!' Zak said. 'As long as you wear that necklace, no magic will work on you. Now if you don't mind . . . I gotta go. *Adios, bambinos!*' He clicked his fingers and winked before vanishing.

'He's *so* cool!' whispered Ella.

'He's *so* annoying!' muttered Cole, Anansi, Hansel and Jack at exactly the same time.

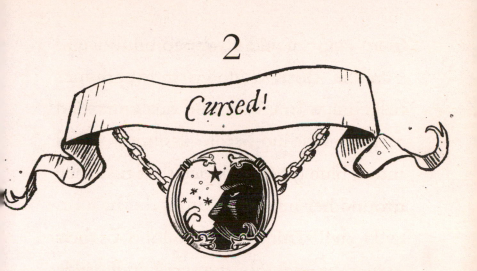

2

Cursed!

Not long after Zak had vanished, everyone went home for tea. Ella and Cole were staying with Rapunzel while they were in Tale Town, although none of them were sure if Rapunzel's parents actually knew about this arrangement. Rapunzel's parents were the King and Queen of Tale Town, so they were always *very* busy – and the palace was so huge that a couple of extra guests could easily go unnoticed.

While they waited for the dinner bell, Rapunzel, Ella and Cole decided to play hide-and-seek. Nobody knew *exactly* how many rooms the palace had – some of the larger bathrooms even had mini-bathrooms of their own – so a single game of hide-and-seek could last for *weeks*.

'Twelvety-nine, twelvety-ten, *fifty*!' shouted Cole, who struggled a bit with some of the larger numbers. 'Coming, ready or not!'

———◆———

As Cole roamed the corridors, Rapunzel found the perfect hiding spot. It was a huge urn on the landing of the East Wing's staircase. At first she

thought about
climbing
inside, but
it seemed a
bit wobbly,
so she squeezed
in behind it instead.
It was very dusty, and just as she was
pulling her incredibly long hair out
of sight, she sneezed a HUGE sneeze,
bumping her head against the urn.

'*Ouch!*' muttered Rapunzel, then
added, 'Oh no!'

The urn wobbled . . . forward . . .
and backwards . . . until with a hollow
THUNK it toppled over and tumbled
down the stairs.

'Perhaps it'll be OK?' thought

Rapunzel, as the urn bounced away.

There was a horrible crashing sound.

'Oh . . .' she thought, looking at the hundreds of tiny, broken pieces. 'Perhaps not.'

———◆———

Rapunzel was wondering what to do about it when her parents crossed the hallway, followed by a group of palace staff and a small army's worth of suitcases. They were *bound* to see the broken urn.

'Ah, *daaahling*! There you are!' purred Rapunzel's mother. 'I'm so glad we've bumped into you. I'm afraid that Daddy and I have to go away on *urgent* official business.'

Rapunzel inspected their luggage.

One case in particular looked rather like a set of skis. 'Urgent skiing business?' she asked.

'That's right, my petal!' exclaimed her father. 'Ruling Tale Town can be *exhausting* and I need to unwind! Why, the journey home from last week's scuba-diving trip has left me worn out! Your governess will look after you while we're away.' He glanced over at his wife. 'You *did* tell the governess, didn't you, darling?'

'I thought we'd fired her?' said the Queen.

'So we did!' exclaimed the King, laughing. He turned back to Rapunzel, 'Anyway, the palace has got *lots* of servants. Just call for them if you need food or someone to get you dressed.'

'I can dress myself!' said Rapunzel.

'That's the spirit!' replied her father, clapping her on the back. 'Anyway, must dash, there's a boat waiting. Love you! Byeee!' He turned to walk down the stairs, his feet crunching on the broken urn.

'What the blazes!' he exclaimed. 'Does *anyone* EVER do any cleaning around here?'

Rapunzel's face started to feel hot.

'What *on earth* has happened to the urn from the landing?' asked the Queen, her eyes narrowing. '*Rapunzel?*'

'Ah . . . well . . . you see . . .' started Rapunzel.

'Yes?' said her parents.

Rapunzel didn't *really* mean to say what came out of her mouth next, but that didn't matter, because she said it anyway.

'It was Ella,' said Rapunzel in a rush. 'You know, the girl who's been staying here? We were playing hide-and-seek and she *accidentally* broke it. I was just trying to see if I could fix it. She's *very* sorry – so *please* don't be cross with her.'

There was a moment's pause as Rapunzel's father looked at his watch, and her mother looked between Rapunzel and the broken urn.

Rapunzel held her breath.

'I never liked that urn anyway!' said the Queen. 'A ghastly pattern and an ugly shape – utterly *horrible!*'

'But, darling!' protested the King, 'I gave you that urn on our wedding day!'

'Really?'

'Yes! As a symbol of my undying love.'

'Well, it just goes to show what *horrible* taste you have!' Rapunzel's mother laughed, patting her husband on the arm. 'Now come along, we don't want the boat to leave without us. See you *sooooon*!' she cooed to Rapunzel, and then they were gone.

——— ◆◆ ———

Rapunzel let out a deep breath and muttered, '*That* was lucky.' She was about to look for someone to clear up the mess when she was startled by an angry voice.

PHEW!

'I don't know what *you're* so happy about!' it said.

'Who's that?' gasped Rapunzel. She spun around

but there was nobody there. Then a small teapot on a nearby shelf wobbled as a head popped out of the top and wings sprouted from the sides.

'*I* am a hermit genie, and it was *my* home that you just *destroyed*!' shouted the strange creature. 'I *loved* that urn! Spent the best years of my life in it – and *now* what? I'm living in a *teapot*!'

'Ah . . .' said Rapunzel. 'Sorry!' She'd heard about hermit genies – they lived in empty bottles, urns, lamps and, occasionally, shoes. They could only leave their homes for a few seconds, so if they had to move house in a hurry, they didn't get long to find somewhere new.

'Oh, you're "sorry", are you?'

growled the hermit genie, flapping his wings so hard the teapot hovered in mid-air. 'Well *that* won't do *me* much good! Not now I'm stuck living in a teapot! Nobody will *ever* take me seriously wearing *this*.'

'Oh, it's not that bad!' replied Rapunzel. 'It's quite pretty actually. And it must be loads lighter – there's no way you could have flown around carrying that massive urn.'

'That's not the point!' snapped the genie, his pointy beard trembling with fury. 'The *point* is that you broke my home and *then* you lied!'

'Well, I've said I'm sorry!' said Rapunzel. 'What more do you want?'

The genie gasped. 'What *more*?

How about a nice Ming vase to live in? Or a *real* apology, one that you *actually* mean!'

Rapunzel looked at the genie thoughtfully. 'Hang on. As you're a genie, aren't you meant to offer me some wishes or something?'

'I *cannot* believe your cheek!' spluttered the genie. '*Someone* needs to teach you some manners, young lady—'

'OK . . . look, I'm sorry,' interrupted Rapunzel. 'I *promise*. Now, let's start over. We've got an Ancient Urns and Exciting-Looking Lamps, Jars and Bottles room somewhere in the palace. You can pick whichever one you like.'

'It's *too late* for that now!' said the genie coldly. 'You broke my home and blamed it on your friend! You think you can get away with *anything* – but no more! From now on every single thing that goes wrong in Tale Town will be blamed on . . . YOU!' The genie popped out of the teapot and waggled his hands in Rapunzel's direction. *'This is my curse: the spell has been spun, so it will stay till your crime is undone!'*

'No! Wait! Stop!' shouted Rapunzel, but the teapot and the genie had vanished in a puff of purple smoke. 'Oh well,' she muttered as she walked to the kitchens to find someone to clear up the broken urn. 'How bad can it be?'

3

Blame-storm

'**Y**OU!' shrieked the cook, the moment
Rapunzel pushed open the door to
the busy palace kitchens. 'YOU made
the milk go sour!'

Rapunzel yelped in surprise. 'What?'
she protested. 'I just got here. I don't
even know where you keep the milk!'

'A likely story!' muttered the cook.
'I know it's *your* fault!' She jabbed a
stubby finger at Rapunzel's chest.

'*Oh no . . .*' groaned Rapunzel. 'It's the hermit genie's spell!'

At the far end of the room, a kitchen boy was carrying a huge bucket of muddy vegetables. He tripped over his shoelace and fell, scattering dirty potatoes all over the floor.

'Now look what you've done!' yelled the cook, glaring at Rapunzel.

'Seriously?' said Rapunzel. 'I was nowhere *near* him! How could I have tripped him over?'

'That doesn't matter,' said the cook. 'What matters is . . .' She paused, looking confused. 'You made me forget what I was going to say! *Witchling!*'

'Rapunzel just made me cut my thumb!' yelled the pastry chef from a table nearby.

'And she burned my bread!' shouted the baker, holding up a blackened loaf.

'*Whatever,*' muttered Rapunzel, backing out of the room as the kitchen boy, cook, pastry chef and baker all shouted after her.

Rapunzel wanted to find Ella and Cole to explain what had happened, but every time she saw *anyone*, they blamed her for something that she hadn't done. In the end she had to hide in the room where her parents stored all the letters of complaint from the people of Tale Town – nobody *ever* went in there.

Rapunzel crouched among the huge piles of angry letters as she listened to the palace staff shouting about all the things she had supposedly done wrong. 'Everyone in this place is *totally* mean!' she sulked. 'That's it! I'm getting out of here!' And with that she climbed out of the window using her long, golden hair.

The trouble with magic
is that you *can't* run away from it.
No matter where Rapunzel went,
someone was trying to blame her for
something. Humpty Dumpty was
saying she had pushed him
off a wall. An elderly
couple were telling
everyone that she
had made their
gingerbread
man run off,
leaving them
without a tea-
time snack. And –
worst of all – a huge
crowd was standing around a particularly smelly pile of horse poo in the

middle of the street, looking at Rapunzel and shaking their heads in disgust.

'THAT was *definitely* not me!' cried Rapunzel as she ran off to look for Red. Maybe *she'd* be able to help?

'So!' barked Red as she opened her front door. 'Have you come to say sorry?'

'What for?' asked Rapunzel.

'For making me spoil my picture!' said Red, holding up a soggy piece of paper with some smudged lines on it. 'You made me spill my drink when you knocked at the door!'

'Come on, Red!' exclaimed Rapunzel. 'How could I be coming to say sorry, if it was the knocking that made you spill your drink?'

There was a crash from the garden. Red's dad was chopping large bits of wood into smaller bits, which he'd eventually glue back into large pieces to chop all over again. It was what he liked to do on the weekends when he didn't have any *real* woodcutting to do.

'Tell Rapunzel to leave my tools alone!' shouted Red's dad. 'She broke the handle on my favourite axe. It could have caused a nasty accident!'

'And *another* thing!' added Red crossly. 'Jack told me that Betsy's caught chicken pox – and he said it was *you* that gave it to her!'

'What?' said Rapunzel. 'Can chickens even *get* chicken pox?'

They were interrupted by a ferocious

roar from deep within the forest. A distant voice screamed: 'Rapunzel's set a bear loose in the forest! *RUN!*' This was followed by another roar and an even louder scream. '*MY LEG!*' the voice cried again. '*Rapunzel owes me a new leg!*'

Red glared at Rapunzel. 'Why are you doing all this?' she hissed, then slammed the door in her friend's face.

Rapunzel stood there in shock until

WHO'S BEEN EATING MY PORRIDGE?

the sound of the bear got too close for comfort. If her best friend wouldn't help her, who would? As she ran away, she thought about what the hermit genie had said: '*So it will stay till your crime is undone!*'

Somehow she had to *undo* what she had done – *but how?*

Suddenly it all became clear. She needed to find the urn and glue it back together! That was *bound* to work. Now she just had to get back into the palace without being seen . . .

4

Bad Heir Day

After using her magical plaits to climb up to her bedroom window at the top of the tallest tower, Rapunzel dashed through the palace to the East Wing staircase, wearing a large hooded cloak to hide her face and hair. But she was too late! The broken urn had been cleared away.

'What am I going to do?' gasped Rapunzel. Since her only magical power was her really, *really* long hair, which was super-glossy, looked *amazing* in photographs and was great for climbing, things weren't looking great.

She was starting to panic when a voice called out, 'Ah-ha! Found you!'

'What? Who? Where? *I didn't do it!*' blurted Rapunzel.

'Didn't do *what*?' asked Ella. 'I thought we were playing hide-and-seek?'

'So, you don't think . . . um, that it's all my fault?' asked Rapunzel.

'*What's* all your fault?'

You know . . . *Everything?*'

'Er . . . no. Why should everything be your fault?'

'It *shouldn't*! That's the point!' cried Rapunzel. She noticed Ella's blue glass

necklace and breathed a sigh of relief
as she remembered Zak's spell — magic
didn't work on Ella! Finally, she had
someone on her side.

◆

'Look, this is what happened . . .'
explained Rapunzel. 'A moody old
hermit genie got cross with me and

now I'm cursed! I'm being blamed for *everything* that goes wrong in the whole of Tale Town — even if it couldn't *possibly* be my fault!'

'But why on earth would a hermit genie do *that*?' asked Ella, her eyebrows crinkling in concern.

Rapunzel felt her face go red. 'I'm not sure,' she muttered. 'But he's *totally* got it in for me! Now everyone hates me!'

'Oh, poor you!' exclaimed Ella. 'That must be awful!'

Rapunzel shifted her feet uncomfortably.

'Still, that explains why Cole was acting so strangely. He stormed off to the Fairy Folk Forest saying that you'd hidden all of his clean pants, and he *never* wears clean pants anyway!'

Rapunzel sighed. 'That sounds about right.'

'So what are you going to do?' asked Ella.

'I don't know,' replied Rapunzel. 'I guess I'll—'

She was interrupted by an alarm ringing out through the castle. It was an alarm that everyone knew, and everyone hoped they would never hear.

Trolls were attacking Tale Town.

<hr />

Rapunzel and Ella crept out of the palace to try and find out what was happening, the wailing of the siren echoing through the cool evening air.

Rapunzel pulled the hood of her cloak forward so her face was hidden. 'What's going on?' she hissed.

'I don't know,' replied Ella. 'But it sounds like it's something to do with the Story Tree.'

'The *Story Tree*?' gasped Rapunzel.

'I'll try to find out more,' said Ella. 'Stay out of sight!' She darted off, pushing her way through the mass of confused townsfolk.

A short while later Ella returned –

her eyes wide. 'The trolls tried to set fire to the Story Tree!' she said. 'The good news is they were chased away before the tree caught fire – although the town hall *is* burning down.'

'If that's the good news, then what's the *bad* news?' asked Rapunzel.

Ella looked uneasily at her friend as the angry roaring of the crowd became clear:

'It's *HER* fault!'

'RAPUNZEL!'

'She led them here!'

'She's a troll spy!'

'Oh,' said Rapunzel, turning pale.

'*That's* kind of the bad news,' said Ella. 'Perhaps we should get out of here?'

Rapunzel and Ella had been running for *ages*. They'd run far beyond the town walls and deep into the woods. As they had been sneaking out of town, Ella had spotted Jack, Hansel and Gretel in the crowd, but as soon as she'd said she was trying to help Rapunzel, Jack had yelled: '*HEY! EVERYONE! Rapunzel's over here – she's the one in the big hood! She made me forget my seven-times table!*' and Betsy had added a VERY cross-sounding, '**WHAAAAAT!?!**'

'Don't you worry, Betsy –'

'– she won't get away with it!' yelled Hansel and Gretel.

After that, it seemed like

all of Tale Town had started chasing them! It was only luck that had kept them ahead of the crowd, but now Rapunzel's legs were burning and Ella was gasping for breath.

'Quick! Let's hide in there!' wheezed Ella, pointing to an old cart she'd spotted, hidden in a small clearing. The small wagon stood in the shadows, almost entirely concealed by bushes.

'It doesn't look very clean . . .' muttered Rapunzel, poking at the animal skins which filled the back of the cart. She wrinkled her nose.

'It doesn't *smell* very clean either!'

'Oh, come on!' hissed Ella. 'Staying clean is the least of our worries!'

Rapunzel paused. Ella was right, but the cart really did smell *awful*. 'Thanks for helping me, Ella,' she said. 'But can't we—'

'You're welcome!' interrupted Ella. 'Now *in you get!*' She shoved Rapunzel into the cart and jumped in too, covering them both in the smelly skins.

'Now what?' hissed Rapunzel.

'Now . . . we wait,' whispered Ella. 'Stay quiet! I can hear them coming!'

5

More Haste, Less Speed

'Whass goin' on?' Rapunzel muttered blearily. There was a heavy weight on her stomach and the floor *kept* banging into her head. 'Stop it!' she mumbled, trying to sit up. She felt very hot, a bit queasy and *something* smelt *awful*. She shoved the weight off her stomach and a voice murmured, 'Hey! Watch it!'

It was Ella! Of course! They'd been

hiding in the cart! They must have fallen asleep. Rapunzel threw off the animal skins and looked around. They were bouncing down a forest path she didn't recognize.

She turned to Ella and they both jumped when a deep voice boomed out, 'Ella? Rapunzel? What in the Fairytale Kingdom are *you* doing here?'

'Well, I'm sorry to hear all that,' said Anansi's Uncle Rufaro, once Rapunzel and Ella had explained what had happened. 'It's a good job I wasn't in Tale Town at the time, or the genie's spell would have worked on me, too!' He scratched his huge green jaw with an equally huge green hand. 'Listen,

I've got a *very* important meeting later today,' he added in his rumbling troll voice. 'It's to do with the curse on my family – I *have* to go – and there's no way that I could take you back to Tale Town and *still* get there in time. I'm really sorry, girls, but you're going to have to come along.'

'Fine with me,' said Rapunzel. 'I'm not exactly flavour of the month at home.'

'And I'm staying with Rapunzel until she gets rid of this curse,' added Ella.

'Well, that's settled then,' said Rufaro. 'But you'd better let the palace know you're OK – they'll be sending out search parties and all sorts!'

'More like angry mobs . . .' muttered Rapunzel. Even so, she agreed to send a note wrapped around the leg of one of the tame birds that flew through the forest.

Dear Palace Staff,

Hello. I am perfectly fine – not that you'd care! Last time I saw any of you, I was being chased with flaming torches and pitchforks! The attack on the Story Tree was nothing to do with me! Just you wait until this spell is broken ... We are going to have serious words!

Obviously I'm not going to tell you where I am – but I'm safe and with friends.

Not very fond wishes,

Rapunzel

They watched as the pink little bird took flight, dancing through the air and tweeting out little heart-shaped musical notes.

'How *do* they do that?' marvelled Rapunzel as the bird flew off to Tale Town. She turned to face Rufaro. 'So anyway, who's this person that you're meeting later? Won't they be a bit surprised when a troll turns up?'

Rufaro looked worried. 'Um, I probably should have told you earlier,' he muttered. 'The person I'm meeting is a troll . . . in the middle of a field full of trolls . . . at a giant troll market just outside of Goatbridge.'

'Well *that's* just *fantastic!*' said Rapunzel in a *That's-not-really-very-fantastic-at-all* sort of way. 'Do you think we can get that bird back?' she added. 'I need to

cross out the line where I wrote
"I'm safe".'

* * *

The cart bounced uncomfortably as
it trundled slowly through the forest.
Rufaro looked anxiously at his watch.

'Can't the horses go any faster?'
asked Ella.

Rufaro shook his head. 'They've not had a rest since I set off last night – they're exhausted, poor things.'

'I know!' exclaimed Ella. 'Maybe Cole can help, he's *always* got a couple of tricks up his sleeve.'

Rufaro frowned. 'Are you sure?' he asked. 'You know his magic can be . . . unpredictable?'

'How *DARE* you!' yelled Cole as he fizzed into view, inches away from Rufaro's face. 'It's only because of *RAPUNZEL* that my spells aren't working properly.' He glared at her angrily. 'I don't know how you did it, but you'd better fix my magic – *and soon*!'

'Come on, Cole!' said Ella soothingly. 'It's not Rapunzel's fault! You only *think* that it was because of the hermit genie's horrid curse!'

'Whatever,' muttered Cole. 'What's the problem anyway? You want to speed this journey along?' He looked at the trees that they were *very* slowly passing by. 'I can do that, *no problem!*'

Before Rufaro could stop him, Cole performed his spell-making dance. He flung his arms into the air, screwed up his face and danced around as though he was trying to shake off his pants without removing his trousers. His hands quivered and his eyes shone bright with wild, blue magic.

'It's done!' he exclaimed happily. 'The horses will go faster now – just you wait!'

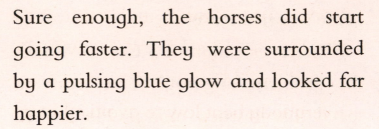

Sure enough, the horses did start going faster. They were surrounded by a pulsing blue glow and looked far happier.

'I was wrong!' Rufaro laughed. 'Good job, Cole!'

The wind whipped through Rapunzel's hair as the cart went faster and faster. 'Wow!' she said. 'We'll be there in no time at all . . . *Duck!*'

'What—' began Ella, but was cut off as a leafy branch slapped into her face. Overhanging branches and leaves were shooting past faster and faster. Cole grinned proudly, but Rufaro frowned as he tried to keep control of the cart.

'Cole, is there any way we can slow

this down a bit?' the troll asked.

'Make your mind up!' exclaimed Cole.

'*Duck!*' cried Rapunzel.

Everybody bent low to avoid a heavy branch that whipped over their heads. Rufaro grimaced as he pulled on the reins in a desperate attempt to keep the cart on the road.

'Cole!' yelled Rufaro. 'We need to—'

'*DUCK!*' shouted Rapunzel.

WHACK!

Rufaro and Ella ducked down again – then sat up, looking confused. There weren't any low branches nearby.

'NO! I mean *that* duck – *over there!*' yelled Rapunzel, pointing at a very worried-looking duck up ahead in the middle of the path.

Rufaro yanked the reins and the cart swerved to the left. They sped past the duck, which let out an angry 'QUUUUUACK!' as the cart zigzagged all over the road, skipping and bouncing, completely out of control.

Rapunzel, Ella and Rufaro screamed as the cart went up on two wheels, then tipped over completely, scattering broken wood, animal furs, two girls, one fairy and a troll into the woods.

6

Unfinished Monkey Business

'Hmm . . .' said Rufaro as he looked from Cole to the broken cart and back to Cole again.

'Stupid Rapunzel, breaking everything,' muttered Cole.

Rufaro's eyebrows knotted together. '*Hmm . . .*' he said once more, although this time it was more of a growl.

Everyone looked at the splintered wood that had once been Rufaro's

cart, and at the scattered animal furs it had been carrying.

'Well . . .' said a voice from deep within the trees. '*That* doesn't look good.'

'Who's there?' shouted Rufaro, moving Ella and Rapunzel safely behind him. 'Show yourself!'

'OK!' replied the voice. There was a swooshing sound as a small green blur shot through the air above, swinging through the trees like a gymnast before landing gracefully in front of them and doing a little bow.

'You're . . . you're a *monkey*!' said Rapunzel.

The monkey nodded.

'You're . . . a small, *green* monkey,'

added Ella, stepping out from behind Rufaro.

Again, the monkey nodded. 'And *you* have two working eyes,' he replied. 'Pleased to meet you, I'm Alphege.' He held out his hand and Ella bent down to shake it.

'Nice to meet you. I'm Ella.' She gestured around their small group. 'This is Rapunzel, Rufaro and Cole.' Everybody waved, then fell into an awkward silence.

'So, can all of your family talk?' Ella asked politely. 'I've never met a talking monkey before.'

Alphege grinned. 'Of *course* my family can talk, but then again, they *are* human.'

'Well *you* must have come as quite a surprise!' said Rapunzel.

Alphege burst out laughing. 'It's a curse!' he explained. 'I'm human too! I wasn't *born* like this. Anyway, it looks like you need some help?'

'Well, it's kind of you to offer,' said Rufaro. 'But unless you have some sort of horse-drawn carriage, then I don't see how . . .'

Alphege put two green fingers into his mouth and blew a shrill, ear-piercing whistle. Two large brown monkeys swung down from the trees and chattered at Alphege, waving their hands and slapping the floor. Alphege shook his head crossly, chattering and shrieking before baring his teeth, beating his chest and pointing into the undergrowth. The monkeys bowed low and sprang away.

'What was *that* all about?' asked Ella.

Alphege sighed. 'Well, they were asking if I wanted spaghetti hoops for dinner, but I told them that I *HATE* spaghetti hoops.' His little green face looked extremely cross. 'I've *always* hated spaghetti hoops, they *really* should know that by now!'

'And that helps us *because* . . . ?' asked Rufaro.

'Oh yes,' continued Alphege. 'Sorry — I *also* ordered them to ready the carriage and bring it here *immediately*. I probably should have said: I'm kind of the King around here.' He grinned proudly. 'I *think* it's because of the green fur!'

Moments later, a carriage woven from thin branches burst through the trees with a thunderous crash and stopped just in front of them. Ella and Rapunzel looked on with wide eyes: instead of horses pulling the carriage, a team of four gorillas stood there, with special harnesses around their huge chests.

'Marvellous work!' exclaimed Alphege, swinging up on to Ella's shoulder and standing on tiptoes to clap one of the gorillas on the back. Then he turned back to the others and smiled. 'Ladies and gentlemen – your carriage awaits!'

Ella, Rufaro and Rapunzel bounced around inside the carriage as they sped through the forest. Alphege was perched on Rapunzel's shoulder, staring at her silken hair, while Cole was outside, keeping the gorillas company. This was partly because he wanted some fresh air, but mainly because Rufaro had made it clear that if Cole didn't STOP telling his 'jokes', then 'bad things' were going to happen.

'Here's the plan,' said Rufaro. 'Once we get there, you all wait at the edge of the forest while I go into the market. I've brought all the goatskins from my wagon so I'll look like a trader and nobody will ask any questions. As soon as I've found the troll I'm meeting and got the information I need, I'll come straight back. Whatever happens, I *must* get back before it gets dark, as I'll turn back into a human in the moonlight. Can you imagine what would happen then?'

'They'd eat you,' said Alphege. 'Or maybe just capture you, or—'

'I didn't *really* expect you to answer the question!' interrupted Rufaro.

'So what if something goes wrong?' asked Ella.

'Nothing's going to go wrong,' said Rufaro.

'But what if they find out you're not *really* a troll?' asked Rapunzel.

'Listen,' said Rufaro. 'The most important thing is that you all stay safe. If I'm not back by nightfall . . . well . . . Alphege can take you home.'

Rapunzel frowned. 'But you

haven't answered my—'

'Do you mind if I add a little something?' interrupted Alphege. 'It's just I think your plan has one *teeny* problem . . .'

'And that is?' asked Rufaro.

'*It's terrible!*' exclaimed Alphege.

Rufaro sighed.

'How about this?' Alphege continued. 'You and I go in *together*. You can pretend to be a street performer, and I'll be your dancing monkey. That way you'll have some backup . . . just in case!'

Rufaro frowned. 'I suppose that *does* make sense . . .'

Alphege grinned. 'Cole should come too. Then if we *do* get into trouble he can fly out and tell Ella, Rapunzel, Professor Hendricks and the others, so they can rescue us!'

'And Professor Hendricks is . . . ?' asked Ella.

'One of the gorillas,' explained Alphege. 'They're all *very* well educated – what they don't know about science, art and history isn't worth knowing. So, what do you think?'

'I'm not sure about getting the girls involved,' said Rufaro.

'*Because?*' said Rapunzel, glaring at him.

'Well . . . it's just . . .'

'Because we're *girls?*' said Ella, narrowing her eyes.

'No!' replied Rufaro.

'I'd just be happier knowing you're out of harm's way.'

'Seriously?' asked Rapunzel, using her best *I'm-a-princess-and-you'd-better-not-be-arguing-with-me* voice. 'You do remember how Ella and I met? When *we* rescued *your* sister from a wicked witch?'

Rufaro shuffled uncomfortably.

'Besides, have you seen the size of these guys?' added Ella, pointing at the gorillas pulling the carriage. 'They'll be here if we need any muscle.'

'Absolutely,' said Alphege. 'And while you're waiting, they're *very* good company, especially Dr Newton – she's a laugh a minute! Although as you don't speak ape, I guess it'll all just sound like grunts.' He shook his head sadly. 'So, are we agreed?'

Rufaro sighed again and nodded.

'Excellent!' cried Alphege as he picked something from Rapunzel's hair and popped it into his mouth. 'Let's *do this thing*!'

'Did . . . did you just take something out of my hair and . . . *eat it*?' asked Rapunzel.

'Sorry, I forgot myself for a minute,' said Alphege. 'Don't worry, it was only a flea.'

'I do *NOT* have fleas!' shouted Rapunzel.

'Oh, I know,' said Alphege. 'It was one of mine – I'd recognize them anywhere.'

'Aarghh! Get off!' shrieked Rapunzel, batting Alphege off her shoulder. 'There is *NO WAY* that *I'm* getting *fleas!*'

'Enough!' interrupted Rufaro. 'This is serious, OK?'

They all nodded and fell silent.

Ella tried not to smile as she noticed Alphege sneakily pick up the very end of Rapunzel's plait, pick something off it, and pop it quickly into his mouth.

7

A Deal's a Deal

'What's happening?' hissed Rapunzel. Ella was peering through a pair of Alphege's home-made binoculars. They were high in a tree, overlooking the open-air market at Goatbridge. It was well over an hour since Rufaro, Cole and Alphege had gone in, and the sun was already hanging low in the sky.

'I don't know!' replied Ella. 'It's

really busy — I can't see them *anywhere*. Wait . . . Over there!'

'Where?' asked Rapunzel, grabbing the binoculars. At first, all she could see was brightly coloured tents and trolls, until Ella guided the binoculars to the left and she saw Alphege dancing on the top of an upturned barrel, wearing a waistcoat and a little hat with a tassel on. He did *not* look happy.

'What should we do?' asked Ella.

'Nothing . . . *yet*,' replied Rapunzel. 'If they need our help they'll send Cole.'

———◆———

The early evening sun sliced across the market with a warm pink light. The sound of laughter and music rang out as hundreds of trolls wandered around,

chatting and
joking with
each other.

Alphege was
hopping from foot
to foot on his barrel,
beating a little drum
and occasionally
trying (and failing) to
ride a tiny blue
unicycle. Before they'd entered the
market, Rufaro had asked Cole to
disguise himself, and although turning
into a miniature unicycle had seemed a
rather odd choice at first, it *had* come in
very useful. Each time Alphege fell off,
the trolls burst out laughing and Rufaro
encouraged him to do it again.

Despite the carnival atmosphere, Alphege was *not* having fun. He *hated* being laughed at, and was just about to storm off for a good sulk when a huge, mean-looking troll joined the audience. He grinned at Rufaro – with lots of jagged teeth, but no warmth at all. 'What do we have here?'

exclaimed the troll. 'Why, it's a couple of dancing monkeys!'

'OK, folks!' bellowed Rufaro, grabbing Alphege by the scruff of his neck and swooping up the blue unicycle. 'The show's over now, thank you!'

The mean-looking troll placed a muscular arm around Rufaro's shoulders and steered him away from the crowd. 'Interesting,' he muttered. 'It's *very* convincing. Hardly anyone would be able to tell that you're actually *human*.'

He raised his voice on the word 'human' and Rufaro winced.

'So, have you got what I asked for?' asked the troll, smiling his cold smile.

'Right here . . .' said Rufaro, holding up a sack. The troll grinned and reached out, but Rufaro pulled the sack away. 'Not yet,' he said. '*First* you need to give *me* what *I* came for.'

'Fine,' rumbled the troll, looking at Alphege and licking his lips. 'But I'm *far* too hungry to talk right now. You'll get what you want – *after* I've eaten . . .'

Rufaro looked around at the lengthening shadows and took a deep breath. 'All right,' he agreed, 'but make it quick. I'm in a hurry.'

'I know *just* the place,' said the troll, staring unpleasantly at Alphege.

———— ◆ ————

Professor Hendricks, Dr Newton and the other gorillas had joined Ella and Rapunzel up in the treetops. The last of the afternoon light was fading and *everyone* was starting to feel nervous.

'Where are they now?' asked Ella.

'In some sort of tent,' replied Rapunzel, who was holding the binoculars. 'That big troll led Rufaro in there, and now I can't see *anything*!'

'What should we do?' asked Ella.

Professor Hendricks grunted deeply, snorted, scraped the back of his hand across the side of his face and made a sound like 'Ooooh-ooooh-oooooooh!' He looked expectantly at Ella.

'I'm really sorry, but I've got *no idea* what

you're saying,' said Ella. Professor Hendricks rolled his eyes, then traced a few letters on to the branch in front of them:

P A N I C ?

'Now is *not* the time for panicking!' snapped Rapunzel. 'I thought Alphege said you guys were smart?'

Professor Hendricks blew a raspberry, then traced a few more letters out:

I ' M A
S C I E N T I S T
N O T A
S O L D I E R !

'Let's at least get the carriage ready,'

said Ella. 'I've got a feeling we might need it.'

———— ◆ ◆ ————

Inside the dimly lit tent, a large pot boiled away over an open fire. Although most of the smoke escaped through the top of the tent, the air was thick, humid and smelly. Alphege glanced over at Rufaro, whose face was shiny with sweat. They were running out of time.

Slowly, very quietly and without any-body noticing, the small unicycle wheeled itself closer and closer to the door of the tent, and then rolled out into the market and back towards the forest.

'Come *on* . . .' pleaded Rufaro. 'You can't *still* be hungry!'

'Perhaps there's room for one more treat?' the troll said, staring at Alphege. 'I've been thinking. It's a *long* time since we made this deal, and the price has gone up. If you *really* want to hear what I have to say, it'll cost you more monkey!'

'*More* money?' replied Rufaro, shaking his head. 'That's *not* what we agreed.'

'Not *money* . . .' sneered the troll, looking over at Alphege. '*Monkey*!'

'Nope,' replied Rufaro. 'No way – *never* going to happen.'

'Well, I suppose you don't *really* want to know who cursed you, then?' said the troll.

'Surely there's got to be something else?' said Rufaro.

'*Show me the monkey!*' The troll cackled, laughing so hard that he started to cough uncontrollably.

Alphege took the chance to scamper over to Rufaro and tap him on the leg. He winked, nodded and stuck his thumbs up.

Rufaro looked puzzled. He pointed at the troll and mimed someone eating a monkey, but Alphege nodded again and tapped at his head: he had an idea.

'OK then,' Rufaro said out loud to the troll. 'You can have the monkey. But you can't eat it until *after* you give me the information I want.' He pushed Alphege over to the troll and said, 'Tell me what I came here for. Right *now*!'

'Fair enough,' said the troll with a shrug. 'A deal's a deal.'

8

A Daring Rescue

'Now listen up, troops!' barked Rapunzel. 'Here's the drill!' She was marching up and down with her hands clasped behind her back, a look of fierce determination on her face. As soon as Cole had burst through the trees and explained the situation with the troll (which he claimed was all Rapunzel's fault), Rapunzel had leaped into action.

Urmmm...

'We've got two good men in there,' she continued, 'and they need an evac — *pronto!*' Dr Newton slowly raised one huge hairy hand into the air, but Ella leaned in and whispered, 'It's army talk. It basically means we need to get them out — soon!'

Dr Newton smiled gratefully and put her hand down.

'We get this *right*,' continued Rapunzel, 'and we're all on our way back to base for some shut-eye. We get this *wrong*, and it's nighty-night, sleep tight . . . for*ever*!'

Professor Hendricks started to raise his arm but Ella kindly explained, 'What she *means* is that we can't mess this up, or we'll all die. OK?'

Professor Hendricks nodded, but didn't look particularly reassured.

Rapunzel grinned a rather terrifying grin and added, 'OK! Let's bring our boys home!'

<hr />

Back inside the tent, Rufaro was staring at the troll in front of him, with his mouth wide open in shock. 'Did you just say "Hurrilan"?' he asked eventually.

'Yep,' replied the troll. 'It was him, all right. I heard from one of his followers that he'd cursed some humans to look like trolls. I remember being surprised. I mean, who *wouldn't* want to look like a troll? Anyway, Hurrilan is a troll warlock who's been gathering a lot of support in the North. You see, he's got a mix of *all* the different kinds of troll magic: Earth, Air, Fire and Water. It means he has the power to cast really strong spells – *and* to unite the different troll clans. And *that's* just the start of it!'

'What do you mean?' asked Rufaro.

The troll sniggered. '*That*'s not part of the deal. Another monkey might loosen my tongue?'

Rufaro peered out through the gap in the tent at the darkening sky.

'No time . . .' he muttered to himself.
'I've got to go.'

⸻ ◆ ⸻

Rapunzel's plan had sounded OK *at first* – although Ella had been surprised to hear that they were going to pretend to be goats. Especially as Rapunzel had complained so much about even being *near* Rufaro's animal furs in the first place . . .

Once she and Ella were disguised in the skins, they would sneak into the market and create a diversion. Then, in all the chaos, they'd find Rufaro and Alphege. Finally, Professor Hendricks and the apes would charge in with the carriage to get them out of there, and they'd *all live happily ever after.*

Now that she was clinging desperately to the bottom of a cart that was rolling into the market,

Ella decided it was an *awful* plan. Still, it was too late for regrets now.

After what seemed like forever, the cart stopped and Ella dropped heavily to the ground, rubbing her aching arms. Rapunzel had tied herself in place with her hair and smiled at Ella as the knots magically untied themselves and she slid gently down.

'I told you it would work,' Rapunzel whispered with a grin. 'Now for the *fun* part!'

* * *

'Not staying for food?' asked the troll, grabbing Alphege in one huge hand and striding over to the cooking pot. Rufaro watched helplessly. He had to do *something* . . . but *what*?

The troll held Alphege just above the pot and grinned as he lowered the small green monkey towards the bubbling oil.

A blinding flash of green light filled the tent. Instead of a small monkey being held over the pot, there was now a boy with green hair and a long curling tail! The boy kicked his legs out and knocked the pot over, splashing oil all over the floor.

'Come on, let's go!' yelled the boy, as the troll slipped over in the oil and rolled around, trying and failing to heave himself up.

'Alphege?' spluttered Rufaro 'But . . . *how*?'

'Later!' replied the boy. 'Come on!'

'What about Cole?' cried Rufaro,

looking frantically for the small blue unicycle. 'He was here a minute ago!'

'I'm pretty sure he went to tell the others we're in trouble,' said Alphege, 'because we *definitely* are!' He darted out of the tent, followed by a very confused Rufaro.

<hr />

It hadn't taken Ella and Rapunzel long to realize that creating a distraction at a troll market *wasn't* going to be easy – at least, not without getting discovered. They were already attracting quite a lot of attention in their goat disguises, especially when Rapunzel forgot to walk on all fours. Then Ella had spotted the goat pens – hundreds, possibly thousands of goats were crammed

in there, bleating
occasionally.

'*That* looks like a
better distraction
than getting
me to jump
on a table
and tap-
dance,'
muttered Ella,
glaring at
Rapunzel.

'What?' protested Rapunzel. 'I never said it was my *best* idea, just that it was *an* idea.'

'And *you* couldn't have done the tap-dancing?'

'I can't tap-dance.'

'That's *NOT* the point!'

'Oh, come on!' said Rapunzel. 'Stop wasting time! We're on a mission, remember?'

Rapunzel and Ella quickly opened all the goat pens, and then darted for cover. Seconds later, thousands of goats were leaping, bucking and kicking their way to freedom. They burst through tents, pulling out guy ropes and knocking over tables. Soon the entire market was in complete chaos.

As soon as Rufaro set foot outside the tent, he felt a familiar tingling. 'Not *yet!*' he groaned. He ran as fast as he could, grimacing as he looked up at the moon in the darkening sky. 'Too . . . *late!*' he muttered as, with a surge of magical energy, he turned back into a human.

For a moment the trolls stood staring at Alphege and Rufaro as they ran through the crowd, then a few voices began to yell: '*Humans!*' It wasn't long before all Rufaro could hear was a deafening angry roar as trolls approached from all sides.

'You know what?' whispered Alphege as he and Rufaro ground to a halt, trapped by a circle of trolls. 'I think I might be a *teeny* bit scared . . .'

———— ◆ ◆ ————

'Finding Rufaro in this is going to be *impossible!*' hissed Rapunzel from her hiding place behind one of the tents. One goat was chewing her plait, while another stood next to her, casually dropping little brown pellets of goat poo.

'There are goats *literally* everywhere!'

'I know!' whispered Ella, who was crouched next to her. '*And* trolls!'

A confused yell rang out from across the field and they turned to see a giant blue rabbit in a top hat crashing through the tents, throwing rainbows, cartoon lightning bolts and pink clouds in all directions.

'It's Cole!' shouted Ella. 'It *has* to be!'

From behind the rabbit appeared Alphege's carriage, being pulled by the gorillas. Cole was in the driving seat, whipping his hands around as he cast any spell that popped into his head.

'Cole!' shouted Ella, leaping out from her hiding place. 'Over here!'

The rabbit and the carriage swerved towards them, scattering trolls and goats in its wake. 'You look like you could do with a hand,' said Cole as the carriage screeched to a halt.

'We couldn't find Rufaro and Alphege!' gasped Ella as the girls scrambled in.

'Don't worry – the gorillas are on it!' yelled Cole, casting a new spell which made glowing purple rain fall upward out of the ground. The carriage swung around and moments later Ella could see Rufaro's relieved face as they sped closer. But the carriage wasn't slowing down. In fact it was speeding up.

Trolls, goats and tents shot past in a blur. Suddenly the carriage was thrown to one side as Rufaro leaped on board, landing half in and half out of the doorway. 'Thanks for the lift!' he said as he heaved himself in.

'Where's Alphege?' yelled Rapunzel. 'Is he OK?'

'Oh, I'm fine!' came Alphege's voice from on top of the carriage, his green tail dangling through the window. 'Takes more than a crowd of angry trolls to scare me!'

The gorillas increased their speed

as the carriage burst through a fence, scattering the last few goats, and they didn't slow down until they were safely back in the forest.

9

Flashback

A few hours later they were sitting around a crackling campfire, eating a hearty dinner of tinned pasta shapes. All apart from Cole, who had flitted back to the Fairy Folk Forest to attend to some *very* important business. His brother, Zak, had been interviewed in *Fairy Dreamboat* magazine, where he was quoted as saying:

'Everything about being me is

just totally amazing! Apart from my younger brother – he is *soooo* annoying!'

Cole had, of course, blamed Zak's words on Rapunzel, before vanishing with a magic marker and a plan to draw a moustache on every copy of the magazine that featured his brother's silly, smug face.

———— ◆ ————

Alphege leaned back against a tree trunk, basking in the warm glow of the fire as he scooped up a massive spoonful of pasta shapes.

'I thought you didn't like spaghetti hoops?' said Ella.

'Can't stand them!' replied Alphege. 'But spaghetti hoops and pasta shapes are *completely* different!'

Professor Hendricks rolled his eyes.

'So, is your curse lifted now?' interrupted Rapunzel. 'I mean, you're not a monkey any more?'

Alphege shook his head. 'Here's the deal,' he said. 'Basically I get to look human for one day every week.'

Rapunzel glanced at the curly green tail that poked out from underneath his top.

'*Almost* human,' he added with a grin. 'I can change back and forth as often as I like . . . so long as I'm not a boy for more than twenty-four hours every seven days.' There was a green flash, and the small green monkey was sitting there. A moment later, Alphege turned back into a boy. It was all rather confusing.

'But don't you want to break the curse?' asked Rufaro.

'Not really,' said Alphege. 'It's fun being a monkey, and I still get to be human *sometimes* − it's the best of both worlds!' He spooned up the last of his pasta shapes and licked the bowl clean. 'So, Rufaro,

what did that troll mean when he said
"Hurrilan"? It looked like you knew
who he was talking about?'

Rufaro sighed deeply. 'My sister and
I were friends with him once . . .' he
said. 'But *that* was a long time ago . . .'

'*Come down!*' *yelled Adeola.* '*You're too
high up!*' *Rufaro rolled his eyes: his sister
was always worrying. He was nearly eight
now — practically a grown-up!*

'*It's fine!*' *he replied.* '*There's no tree that
I can't cli—*'

*The branch he was standing on snapped,
and Rufaro found himself tumbling towards
the rocks below. The wind rushed up at him.
Rufaro knew this was going to be bad —
really bad.*

But suddenly . . . *it wasn't.*

The wind seemed to be slowing him down, until he came to a stop, hovering just above the ground.

'What?' he murmured as he opened his eyes and looked around. Peering out from behind some bushes was a small, shy-looking troll.

'You used your magic to save my life!' Rufaro said quietly. 'Wow!'

The troll shrugged and looked away awkwardly. Then Adeola rushed forward and grabbed the troll in a warm hug.

'Thank you!' she said, smiling broadly. 'Thank you!'

'. . . And *that* troll was Hurrilan,' explained Rufaro. 'After that we became friends. Of course, we kept it secret – things weren't *quite* so bad back then, but trolls and humans have never *really* seen eye-to-eye.' He sighed and shook his head sadly. 'Hurrilan was an outcast. Usually, a troll has one type of magic: Earth, Air, Fire or Water – but Hurrilan had a mixture of all four, so he could do a *bit* of each, but not *much* of any. His parents had died when he was young, and his clan of Earth trolls were a bit scared of his powers, so poor Hurrilan ended up living on his own in the woods.'

'*Poor* Hurrilan?' said Alphege. 'I thought it was *him* that cursed you?'

'Well, yes, it is looking that way . . .' agreed Rufaro. 'But back then, we were just children.' He paused. 'I don't think Hurrilan had ever had a real friend before he met Adeola and me. Everything was great, until *Jeremy* got involved.'

'Who's Jeremy?' asked Ella.

'Jeremy Fitch – when I was young he was the mayor's son.'

'But isn't he the *current* mayor of Tale Town?' asked Rapunzel. 'I'm sure I've heard my parents say his name – then one of them usually says "What a *ghastly* man".'

Rufaro nodded. 'Yes, you're right. Anyway, back when I was a young, Jeremy somehow found out that Adeola and I had become friends with Hurrilan. I'll never forget the day that I went to meet Hurrilan and found *Jeremy* instead . . .'

'Hey, Hurrilan!' shouted Rufaro, as he and Adeola ran into the clearing. 'Sorry we're

late, I had to do a few chores!'

'Yeah, he had to clear up all the mud he trampled through the house!' said Adeola.

Rufaro laughed. 'Come out, Hurri!' he called.

There was no reply.

'Looking for someone?' asked a mean voice, as Jeremy Fitch stepped out from behind a tree.

'What are you doing here?' asked Adeola.

'What are YOU doing hanging out with trolls?' retorted Jeremy. 'You know trolls mean trouble!'

'Hurrilan's our friend!' said Rufaro angrily. 'Where is he?'

'Your precious troll's fine,' replied Jeremy. 'He's just through here . . .'

Jeremy led them deeper into the woods. After a while they came to a rough cage made from branches, surrounded by Moonstone. Moonstone was always used for protection from trolls, as the silvery rocks weakened their magic and they hated to be near it.

'What are you doing?' yelled Rufaro, running towards the cage.

Trapped inside and cowering from the sticks that were being poked at him by Jeremy's friends was . . . Hurrilan.

'What you told us to!' said Jeremy with a wide grin. 'YOU told us where to find the troll, we captured it, and now we'll to take it back to your dad – just like YOU wanted . . .'

'What—?' began Rufaro, but a strange wailing sound cut him off. It was Hurrilan. His face was twisted with a mixture of sadness and anger.

'Why?' he roared, glaring through the bars at Rufaro and Adeola. 'I thought we were friends?'

'We are!' said Rufaro. 'Jeremy's lying!

I don't know why — but he is!'

It was too late. Hurrilan didn't seem to be able to hear anything. He wailed again and the air whipped up into a tornado. Mist rolled in through the trees and sparks danced in the air. Jeremy and his friends backed away from the cage, which strained under the force of Hurrilan's magic.

'Why isn't the Moonstone working?' yelled one boy.

'Dunno!' shouted Jeremy, as the wooden sides of the cage bent to breaking point. 'Let's get out of here!'

They turned and ran just as the cage exploded outward. The last thing that Rufaro saw was a heavy piece of wood spinning straight towards him.

'I woke up in the clearing with Adeola beside me,' said Rufaro. 'I'm not sure how long I was knocked out for . . . but it was long enough for Jeremy to ruin our lives!'

'What do you mean?' asked Rapunzel.

'Jeremy ran back and told his father how my family were helping the trolls plan an attack on Tale Town. He'd stolen some of Hurrilan's belongings and a letter he had written to me, asking to meet him in secret in the woods. It all *seemed* very convincing . . . I tried to explain, but nobody

would believe me. The next day, my whole family was banished to Far Far Away. I never saw or heard from Hurrilan again.'

'*We've* got to tell everyone the *truth*!' said Ella crossly. 'Mayor Fitch – I mean Jeremy – blamed you for something that wasn't your fault – and look what happened!

'Rapunzel's parents are the King and Queen – surely *they* can do something about it? They'll *know* it's the truth if *you* tell them – right, Rapunzel?'

'Er, yeah,' said Rapunzel, blushing. 'I'd *never* lie to my parents.' She ate the rest of her pasta shapes in silence, feeling more guilty than ever about blaming Ella for breaking the hermit genie's urn – but how could she tell the truth now?

10

Coming Clean

*T*he sun was rising in the sky as the carriage stopped. Rufaro had driven through the night while Alphege and the girls slept, so he and the gorillas decided to get some rest while the others walked into Tale Town.

It was a cold, crisp morning, but the sun was bright and the air smelt clean. While the two girls walked along the familiar road, Alphege decided to swing up into the treetops and take what he called the 'scenic route'.

'Hey, Ella . . .' Rapunzel started, frowning and chewing on the end of her plait.

'Yeah?' replied Ella with a smile.

'*Nothing* . . .' muttered Rapunzel. This was *impossible*! Ella was *always* so kind and nice. *So* understanding and *so* thoughtful! She would *never* blame someone else for breaking a priceless antique urn. 'Of course,' thought Rapunzel, 'Ella had probably never *seen* a priceless urn before she came to live at the castle, so she'd never have had the chance to break one. In that case, it would be more like Ella breaking, say, a cup or something, and blaming it on someone else. Ella *must* have done something like that before . . .'

Rapunzel sighed. Who was she trying to fool? Ella wouldn't even break a *sweat* and blame it on anyone else. She was just *too* good!

Rapunzel groaned quietly.

'Are you OK?' asked Ella, placing a hand on her friend's shoulder.

'Mnghhh . . .' muttered Rapunzel.

'You seem upset,' added Ella. 'Do you want to talk about it?'

'Mnghhh . . .'

'Come on! It's never as bad as it seems,' said Ella. 'Why, I remember when I was being held prisoner by that wicked witch in a freezing-cold, tiny stone room with no windows, and was

ARGHHHHHhh!!

forced to cook, clean and tidy for *everyone* in the castle without being allowed to eat more than one mouldy piece of bread each day! I mean, *sure*, I got a bit down-in-the-dumps *sometimes*, but I always remembered that someone somewhere was worse off than me, and felt sorry for them instead.'

Rapunzel lifted her head and stared at her friend. '*Seriously?* Are you actually *real*? What could be worse than that?'

'Oh, I don't know,' said Ella

breezily. 'Being slowly lowered into a pot of boiling tar filled with heat-proof piranhas? Something like that?'

'Right . . .' said Rapunzel, taking a deep breath. 'OK. It's like this . . .'

Ella smiled and nodded encouragingly.

'We're here because of me. It's *all* my fault, and—'

'Oh, shush, Rapun—'

'*No!* Let me finish,' said Rapunzel. 'It *is* my fault! The genie cursed me, to teach me a lesson after *I* broke its home – and I deserved it! You see . . .' She swallowed uncomfortably. 'I knocked over the urn that the genie lived in and then . . . then . . .' She put her hands over her face, which had turned pink. 'And . . . *then* I blamed it on you! The genie got *super-cross* and sang this stupid little song: "*This is my curse: the spell has been spun, so it will stay till your crime is undone!*" And he cursed me! I *tried* to undo what I'd done by fixing the urn – but I couldn't! And I *know* that you'd never do *anything* like this in a million years and . . . well, basically . . . I wanted to say –' Rapunzel peeped through a gap in her fingers – '*I'm sorry!*'

There was a long pause. Eventually Ella nodded and said, 'I understand.'

'You *do*?'

'Sure! I blamed the wrong person for something once too!'

'You *did*?'

'Yes! Back in the castle where I was a prisoner. The dragon had a nasty cold, and I was looking after her when she sneezed, and fire shot out, burning the witch's favourite curtains to ashes! I didn't want the dragon to get into trouble, so I said . . .' Ella paused.

'Yes?' encouraged Rapunzel.

'Well, I *blamed* . . .'

'Yes?' repeated Rapunzel.

'*Me!*' gasped Ella, her eyes wide. 'And I know it's so *terribly* wrong to lie, but I just couldn't *bear* the thought of the dragon getting into trouble, as she was so ill and it *was* an accident. So I lied! I *lied*!'

Ella struggled to suppress a sob.

'That is *so* not the same thing!' huffed Rapunzel. 'You basically did a *good* thing and got yourself *into* trouble – I did a *bad* thing to get myself *out* of trouble.'

'Well, it doesn't matter anyway,' said Ella, shrugging.

'It doesn't?'

'Firstly, I accept your apology,' said

Ella. 'And secondly, you've said sorry – you've admitted what you did was wrong! Think about the genie's spell: "*So it will stay till your crime is undone!*" I think this means you've fixed things! You've owned up and told me the truth – the curse has *got* to be broken now!'

'You think?'

'Sure I do!' said Ella, patting her friend on the arm. 'We're nearly back to Tale Town now. Just you wait. Things will be different – you'll see!'

11

Homecoming

$\mathcal{E}$lla was right. Things *were* different
in Tale Town – but not in the way
she'd imagined. They were worse.

Far worse.

The never-ending porridge pot was
overflowing again; somebody had also
set off the never-ending Brussels sprouts
pot – and, worst of all, the never-ending
homework pot. The curse was clearly
still in place, as Rapunzel was being

blamed for *all* of it, and everything else that was going wrong too.

Rapunzel pulled her hood further over her face as they waded knee-deep through a foul-smelling mix of porridge, sprouts and complicated maths problems. Alphege swung down from the trees and with a bright green flash turned back into a boy again.

'This place is crazy!' he said, shaking his head in wonder. 'A minute ago I saw a boy fall over and scrape his knee. He started crying but the tears were like tiny little dogs that leaped away as soon as they came out of his eyes! Unbelievable!'

'Ah, yes . . .' replied Ella. 'That'd be Stewart.'

'OK . . . but that doesn't explain the dogs?' said Alphege.

'*Wolves*, actually.'

'What?'

Ella sighed. 'Did you ever hear the story about the boy who cried wolf?' Alphege nodded his head. 'Well, Stewart's the boy who cried *wolves* – it's a completely different story. Oh, and Alphege?'

'Yeah?'

'Maybe tuck the tail away. It's a bit . . . noticeable.'

'Ahh . . . right! Will do.'

'I don't *understand*!' whispered Rapunzel, who hadn't been paying any attention to their conversation. 'I *told you* what I'd done wrong – I've *said* sorry. The curse should be broken.'

———————◆———————

They walked past a large group of townsfolk listening to a half-eaten gingerbread man explain that he'd gone out for his morning run, as usual, when Rapunzel, disguised as a fox, had pretended to help him across a river and then tried to eat him! Then a frog jumped up on to a log and did a very loud croak. Everybody ignored the frog,* but they *did* agree that it was awful of Rapunzel to trick

* What the croak *actually* meant was that he was a handsome prince but Rapunzel had turned him into a frog.

the gingerbread man.

'I have had enough of this!' hissed Rapunzel. 'We need to find that genie and get him to lift the curse – *NOW*!'

'But *how*?' asked Alphege. 'We've got no idea where this genie is likely to be! I mean, where do genies normally hang out?'

Rapunzel's eyes lit up. 'I think I may have an idea! Come on, let's go!'

An hour later, Ella was dragging a large dirty-laundry basket along the palace corridor towards the Ancient Urns and Exciting-Looking Lamps, Jars and Bottles room. 'Why me?' she grunted as she heaved the heavy basket along. 'Why can't Alphege drag the basket?'

'Because *you* live here!' hissed Rapunzel. 'The palace staff know you. It's no *super-fun* party in here, you know!

It smells *awful* and I keep feeling *someone* picking at my hair.'

'Sorry!' said Alphege apologetically. 'It's an instinct. And by the way, I think that smell might be *you*?'

'You—'

'Shush!' interrupted Ella. 'Someone might hear you!' She heaved the basket into the Ancient Urns and Exciting-Looking Lamps, Jars and Bottles room and shut the door.

Almost immediately Rapunzel and Alphege burst out. 'Remind me never to hide in a laundry basket full of dirty socks again!' exclaimed Rapunzel, who had turned a sort of yellowy-green colour.

'Right,' said Ella, biting her lip and trying not to smile.

'Let's get looking,' Rapunzel continued. 'That genie is *bound* to be in here somewhere!'

They split up and ran around the room, tapping, shaking or polishing each urn, jar, bottle or lamp that they could find. At first they were filled with excitement, but that soon faded to disappointment and then, finally, to *worry*.

———◆———

What seemed like hours later, having checked every item in the huge room, they met up back at the laundry basket.

'It's *no good*!' exclaimed Ella. 'He's not here – or if he *is*, then he's ignoring us.'

Rapunzel's shoulders slumped. 'What am I going to do?' she said in a small voice. 'I'm tired! *And* filthy!' She sniffed. '*And* I smell of goat! I just want everything to go back to normal.'

'Don't worry,' said Ella. 'It's all going to be all right. It always is – eventually!'

Just then, the door swung open and two of the palace cleaners wheeled in a cart piled high with industrial-strength polish, cleaning rags and brushes.

'*You!*' shrieked one of the cleaners, waving his fist angrily at Rapunzel.

'You made me late for work when you broke my alarm clock!'

'Quick!' yelled Alphege. 'Let's go!' He sprang towards the cart and tipped it over, scattering its contents all over the cleaners. By the time they had scrambled to their feet, Ella, Rapunzel and Alphege were gone.

Rapunzel's feet pounded down the palace corridors. She glanced back to see Ella close behind her, with Alphege bouncing up and down on her shoulder.

'Faster!' shouted Alphege, who had turned back into a monkey to make it easier to swing on the chandeliers.

'They're gaining on us!' Following them, throwing cutlery, crockery, bread, cushions and anything else they could find, was a huge mass of palace staff, angrily shouting that everything was *RAPUNZEL'S FAULT.* They dashed into the Queen's Room of Unwanted Gifts, which was piled high with beautiful, expensive, but not *quite* right presents, then sprinted through the Palace Dogs' Dining Room. They'd just burst into the Draughty Spare Room for Visitors Who Have Stayed Too Long when another door flew open and a great mass of angry people poured in, cutting them off.

'There she is!' shouted Anansi, who was at the front of the crowd. 'RAPUNZEL made it rain earlier and my friend Incy-Wincy got washed down a rusty old waterspout and grazed his leg!'

'This way!' yelled Ella, kicking open a secret door in the Draughty Spare Room's bookcase of Not Particularly Interesting Books. They shot down a narrow spiral staircase that led into the servants' passages. Eventually they burst into the kitchens.

'Through here!' gasped Rapunzel. 'There's a way out!' They raced to the heavy kitchen-delivery door, all of them straining to push it slowly open.

Unfortunately for Rapunzel, outside was *another* furious crowd. '**WHAAAAAT!?!**' squawked Betsy from the kitchen garden. '**WhaAaa Whaaat Whaaaat? WHAaAAaAT?**'

* ◆ *

'Let's try again!' shrieked Rapunzel as they struggled to pull the door shut again. Hundreds of footsteps echoed behind them as the palace staff burst into the kitchens. They were *completely* surrounded.

Alphege leaped on to Rapunzel's shoulder and tried to hide in her hair, while Ella and Rapunzel backed slowly into a corner as the crowd poured in. They looked at each other nervously.

'I've got an idea!' whispered Ella. 'What if I take off the magic necklace that Zak made for me and *you* wear it? Maybe that will stop the curse?'

'It's worth a try!' said Rapunzel.

Ella pulled the necklace off, but just as she was handing it to Rapunzel, someone threw a mouldy cabbage. Rapunzel ducked, but the cabbage knocked the necklace from her

hand, and it tumbled to the floor and smashed into tiny pieces.

Rapunzel looked in horror at the blue shards and then back to Ella. 'Sorry, it was an acciden—'

'Did you see *that*?' screamed Ella. 'Rapunzel just broke my magic necklace! It's all *her* fault! And have you *seen* what a mess it is in here? Someone really should do some cleaning!' She looked around desperately for a mop and bucket.

Everyone fell silent as a commanding voice boomed out, 'What the *blazes* is happening in here? Why is *nobody* doing their jobs?' The King and Queen cut through the crowd, until they were face to face with their daughter.

'Mum!' Rapunzel gasped. 'Dad! Thank goodness you're back! You've *got* to help me! Everyone keeps blaming me for things that aren't my fault and . . .' She trailed off as her parents stared at her icily.

'I hope that you're proud of yourself, *young lady*,' snapped the Queen. 'That storm you caused almost sunk our ship! *You* are in *serious* trouble.'

Alphege put his furry little arm around Rapunzel's shoulder as she backed even further into the corner.

12

The Genie's Return

Rapunzel took one last step, flattening herself against the wall as much as she could. There was a loud crash as she knocked over one of the big metal kitchen bins.

'Rapunzel just knocked over my bin!' shouted the cook. 'Right in front of my eyes!' A ripple of angry muttering passed through the crowd until, with a bright purple flash, the genie's head appeared poking out of the top of the bin, along with a pair of muscular arms, which he used to heave the bin the right way up.

'YOU AGAIN!' he bellowed at Rapunzel. 'Haven't you learned your lesson yet?'

'Yes!' gasped Rapunzel. '*Yes*, I have! *Please* make it stop! I've *tried* to make up for it! I *tried* to undo what I'd done! It was *me* who broke your urn! I tried to blame Ella, but *I* did it! See? Now *everyone* knows! I've *already* owned up to Ella, I've said sorry. I can see how selfish I've been — how I've taken *everything* for granted!' She paused for a moment, tears pricking at her eyes. 'I know now that while it *really is* great having the longest, most amazingly

silky and shiniest hair in Tale Town –'
she paused to stroke her hair – 'perhaps,
just *perhaps* there is *more* to life than
having lovely hair? And most of all –'
she sniffed loudly – 'I'm *sorry!*' Then
she burst into floods of noisy tears
while everyone else stood there,
not quite sure what to do or say.

'Whoops, *right*, I see . . .'
said the genie quietly. 'As
it happens, I meant to
lift that curse on the
day I cast it.

After I'd calmed down, I thought it was all a bit over the top – but I must have forgotten to do it! I can be *terribly* forgetful sometimes. Sorry about that!' He clicked his fingers, and added, 'There, it's done now.'

He smiled apologetically at Rapunzel who was wiping her nose on her sleeve and rubbing her red-rimmed eyes.

SNIFFFF!

'So . . .' she said between the last few sobs, 'I didn't *need* to say any of that?'

'Well, no,' admitted the genie. 'I suppose not.'

Everyone was silent for a moment. Then Rapunzel said, 'Well, what I said is true anyway . . .' She paused, then added, '*Especially* the bit about having the best hair in Tale Town!'

Everybody laughed and the angry mob began to dissolve, muttering sheepish apologies, and explaining that there was *no way* they'd have actually *used* the pitchforks or flaming torches they were carrying, and how they weren't *quite* sure what had come over them.

◆

Before long, the only people left in the kitchen were Rapunzel, Ella, Alphege, the genie, and the King and Queen.

'Confounded magic!' blustered the King with a tear in his eye, pulling Rapunzel into a tight hug. 'Making me miss my holiday, and *worse* than that . . . turning me against my own daughter! I'm so sorry, darling.'

'Me too,' said the Queen stroking her daughter's hair. 'I'm *very* proud of you,

Rapunzel. Your brave words have shown me that there *is* more to life than being pretty and having lovely things. And to reward you, I shall buy you *two* new ponies *and* a party frock! But first . . . you need a good bath!'

Rapunzel's parents swept out to continue their royal duties of sitting around and being photographed once in a while.

Ella looked over at Rapunzel with one raised eyebrow.

'They'll *never* change,' said Rapunzel with a smile. 'But I think *I* have!'

'I just wanted to say I'm sorry too . . .' said Ella. 'All of a sudden I felt like *everything* in the world was *your* fault.'

'Don't worry about it,' said Rapunzel.

The genie smiled smugly. 'Well, it was a *particularly* good curse!'

Rapunzel narrowed her eyes.

'Although I can see how perhaps it wasn't *so* great for you . . .' he mumbled. 'Sorry again!'

'That's OK,' replied Rapunzel. 'Now come on, we need to find you a new home, something a bit less . . . *bin-y*.' She smiled at the genie as she picked up the old metal bin and they all set off for the Ancient Urns and Exciting-Looking Lamps, Jars and Bottles room again.

13

Pride Comes Before a Fall

*L*ater on, everybody met up at Greentop's Cafe. Red, Ella and Jack were drinking musical milkshakes, and Betsy was singing along with an enthusiastic chorus of 'WhaAaaaAaa WhaaaT WhaaaaT WhaaaT WhaAaa WHAT?' in a surprisingly tuneful voice.

Anansi was eating a rainbow cake that actually glowed with bright, vivid colours, while Rapunzel, Hansel and

Gretel were playing cards with Cole and Alphege.

Professor Hendricks and the other gorillas were building Alphege a small temporary palace in the woods near Rufaro's hideout. He was planning on staying around for a while – *partly* because he wanted to explore the area, but *mainly* because he felt that Rapunzel's plaits needed *much* more thorough grooming.

Everybody had already said sorry to Rapunzel at least twenty times, and she had considered trying to keep it going a bit longer, but decided *that* was something the *old* Rapunzel would have done. Instead, she just took a bite of the butterfly cake that was hovering in the air in front of her.

That was when the air in the clearing crackled and Cole's brother, Zak, appeared in a flash of blue light, looking wild-eyed and frantic.

'Where is it?' he demanded, looking at Ella.

'Oh, hey, Zak!' said Ella, blushing. She used her dress to wipe some crumbs off the table. 'Er, where's *what*?'

'The *necklace*!' replied Zak. 'You know. The one that stops all magic? I . . . er, need it back.'

'Why?' asked Cole frowning. '*Unless—*'

he gasped – 'it wasn't yours! *You* didn't make the spell – you *took it* from someone else!'

'I did NOT!' Zak yelled furiously at Cole. 'Now just hand it over, OK?' he said more calmly to Ella. He winked at her and swept his hair back for good measure.

'I bet it was Fairy Grandfather's!' exclaimed Cole. He turned to face the others. 'He's kind of scary!' he whispered.

Zak darted over to Ella and realized the necklace was no longer around her neck. '*Arghhhh!*' he screamed. '*What have you done with it?*'

'Well, it got, er, sort of broken . . .' said Rapunzel. 'You see, someone threw a potato and—'

'Wasn't it a turnip?' interrupted Alphege.

'No, it was a cabbage!' added Ella. '*Definitely* — it had that cabbage-y smell to it.'

Zak looked furious. '*I don't care what it was!* Have you got *any* idea what you've done? He's going to be furious, you . . . you . . . *silly girl*!' He spat the last words in such a mean voice that Ella took a step backwards, looking shocked.

There was another flash, brighter and more powerful this time, and a tall old man appeared next to Zak. His long white hair fell in swirls about his shoulders and his blue eyes burned with a furious light. 'Zachary!' he bellowed. 'I trust you kept my necklace safe after you "borrowed" it!'

'I . . . er, well . . . it wasn't me . . . it was her fault!' yelped Zak, pointing at Ella. '*She* broke it, not me!'

'I know full well how the necklace was broken!' boomed Cole's Fairy Grandfather. 'I do, after all have *some* magic!' Zak shrank away as his grandfather continued. '*You* were showing off – *as usual*! Luckily for me, I can easily make another necklace . . .

Unluckily for *you*, I shall be taking away *all* your magic for a MONTH.'

'What? You can't!' Zak gasped.

'I already have,' growled the old man. 'Now apologize to that young lady, and *then* I'm taking you home. You are *grounded*, young man!'

'Sorry,' muttered Zak. There was a crackling flash and both Zak and his Fairy Grandfather vanished.

'Whoa!' said Ella, looking over at Cole. 'Remind me *never* to upset your grandfather – he is absolutely *terrifying!*'

Cole's eyes widened and he put his finger to his lips. 'Shhh!' he hissed. 'You *never* know when he's listening!'

'Well, it serves Zak right, if you ask me!' said Rapunzel.

'I never liked him *anyway*,' added Gretel, ignoring the look she got from Hansel. 'His hair was that bit *too* perfect, if you know what I mean?'

'*Totally!*' replied Ella and Rapunzel, making Anansi and Jack look over at Cole with a smile.

'Well done, by the way!' said Jack to Rapunzel. 'You made it on to the Story Tree! I was walking through town earlier when I noticed a new shoot growing – that's a pretty crazy story!'

'Thanks!' said Rapunzel. 'So . . . the Story Tree wasn't harmed at all by the fire?'

Jack shook his head. 'The spell of protection worked this time — but *why* are the trolls so interested in the Story Tree?'

Rapunzel shrugged. 'I don't know . . . but I *do* know that we need to keep an eye on Mayor Fitch. On the ride back to town, Rufaro told us a story about him that was *not* good.'

Ella nodded and turned to Anansi. 'He *hates* your uncle — it's Mayor Fitch's fault that your whole family had to leave Tale Town all those years ago!'

Anansi narrowed his eyes. 'Do you think that's why the troll on the poster looks like Rufaro? Do you think the mayor knows about the curse?'

'Maybe,' replied Rapunzel. 'But *one* thing's for sure: if there's anyone who can find out what's *really* going on in this town . . .' She paused for a moment and looked round at her friends. 'Then it's us!'

'**Whaaat!**' squawked Betsy loudly, and everyone burst out laughing.

'Oh, Betsy!' chuckled Jack, ruffling the feathers on his pet hen's neck. 'You do say the funniest things!'

The End

Alphege

Strengths: Climbing trees, eating bananas and turning into a green monkey

Weaknesses: A teeny bit too much pride

Likes: Grooming for fleas, tinned pasta shapes and his loyal team of gorillas

Dislikes: Spaghetti hoops, unicycle riding, juggling or anything else that makes him look silly

Zak

Strengths: Excellent posing skills and having eyebrows which are TOTALLY on fleek

Weaknesses: Looking in the mirror too much and always trying to look flawless

Likes: Looking in the mirror, looking at photos (of himself) and looking gooooooooood!

Dislikes: Bad hair days and getting told off by MEAN fairy grandfathers

Professor Hendricks

Strengths: Strength! All Alphege's gorilla crew are seriously buff and very intelligent too

Weaknesses: Despite his size, Professor Hendricks is not particularly brave and very likely to PANIC!

Likes: Doing science experiments, nice cups of tea and studying ancient gorilla history books

Dislikes: Trouble, loud noises and scary things!

Rufaro

Strengths: Anansi's uncle is brave, honest, selfless and generous

Weaknesses: He takes on too many burdens when he should ask for help

Likes: His family and friends and learning the banjo

Dislikes: Being asked to STOP playing his banjo and being cursed to look like a troll in the daylight

Look out for

Coming soon!

Out now!